The Forever Dog

By Bill Cochran

Illustrated by Dan Andreasen

HASHERS

For Mo
—B.C.

For Katrina
—D.A.

The Forever Dog
Text copyright © 2007 by Bill Cochran
Illustrations copyright © 2007 by Dan Andreasen

Manufactured in China.

Library of Congress Cataloging-in-Publication Data
Cochran, Bill, date
   The forever dog / by Bill Cochran ; illustrated by Dan Andreasen.— 1st ed.
    p. cm.
   Summary: Mike and his dog Corky plan to be best friends forever, so when Corky becomes sick and dies, Mike is angry about the broken promise.
   ISBN-10: 0-06-053939-9 (trade bdg.) — ISBN-13: 978-0-06-053939-9 (trade bdg.)
   ISBN-10: 0-06-053940-2 (lib.bdg.) — ISBN-13: 978-0-06-053940-5 (lib. bdg.)
   [1. Dogs—Fiction. 2. Death--Fiction. 3. Promises—Fiction.] I. Andreasen, Dan, ill. II. Title.
PZ7.C63927For 2007
[E]—dc22
2006002501
CIP
AC

Typography by Elynn Cohen   1 2 3 4 5 6 7 8 9 10   ❖   First Edition

Corky was one of those dogs that seemed to be built from other dogs' spare parts. He had short skinny legs, crooked ears, more fur than any one dog deserved, and a scruffy tail that never stopped wagging.

Corky was always happy. He certainly didn't seem to care that no one knew exactly what kind of dog he was. If you asked his owner, Mike, you'd get a simple answer: "He's *my* dog."

Mike's mom brought Corky home when he was only seven weeks old, and Mike loved and cared for that dog from the minute it set paw in his house.

Mike taught Corky where to do his business.

Mike took Corky on walks.
Mike taught Corky to play fetch.

Mike made sure Corky got
enough food and, to be sure,
enough treats.

Corky always slept on Mike's bed.

Sometimes he even slept on Mike's head.

Most of all, Corky was a great listener.
Mike spent a lot of time talking to him.
Even though he knew Corky couldn't talk
back, Mike knew deep down that Corky
understood everything he said.
Mike told Corky secrets.

Mike told Corky jokes.

Mike told Corky how
much he loved him.
Corky liked that.
Mike could just tell.

One day Mike and Corky made a plan. Mike told Corky that the two of them would be best friends forever. Anything and everything that Mike did, Corky would do with him. Forever. That was the plan.

It was their Forever Plan.

And it worked beautifully.

Mike graduated from one year to the next in school. Corky was right there with him.

Playing fetch.

Going on walks.

Sleeping on his head.
Life couldn't have been better.

Until one day, Mike came home from school and Corky wasn't there.

Mike's mom told him that Corky was sick—very sick. There was something wrong with Corky's blood, and he had suddenly become very weak. The vet wanted to keep him at the clinic overnight.

Mike didn't sleep that night. He just kept telling himself, Corky's going to be okay. Corky promised. We have our plan. The Forever Plan. It's not the end of forever yet. We still have the plan.

Lying in bed that night, Mike felt something strange. He felt alone.

The next morning the phone rang. A few moments later, Mike's mom walked slowly into his room. Mike had never imagined he would hear what he was about to hear.

Corky had died. The vet had tried everything, but Corky was just too sick.

Mike didn't believe it. He couldn't believe it.

His heart sank lower than it had ever been before. It hurt, really bad, worse than anything he could ever remember.

The next day, Mike and his parents buried Corky with his favorite ball.

Mike cried. He cried like he'd never cried before.

He couldn't go on walks alone.

He couldn't play fetch without someone to fetch.

He couldn't sleep without a dog on his head.

Then Mike got angry.

Corky had broken his promise.

It just wasn't fair.

What about the plan? What about the Forever Plan?

Mike stayed mad at Corky for almost a whole week.

Mike's mom asked him why he was so angry.

Mike had never told anyone about the Forever Plan until then. He told his mom how he and Corky used to have talks, and how they had made a plan. "A plan to always be together. Forever. It was our Forever Plan, and now Corky broke his promise. He didn't keep with the plan. It makes me mad."

Mike's mom asked him if he remembered when Corky was a puppy. She asked him if he remembered how he'd taught Corky what to do.

Mike remembered.

Mike's mom asked him if he remembered how Corky would fetch the ball.

Mike remembered.

Mike's mom asked him if he remembered how Corky slept on his head.

Mike remembered. And as he remembered, he smiled just a little.

Then Mike's mom asked if he thought he'd ever forget these things.

Mike shook his head no. Never.

"Well, then Corky kept his promise."

Mike didn't understand.

"Corky will be with you forever," she said. "It's just different now. Corky the dog had to go away. But Corky your best friend will be with you forever."

Mike asked, "If Corky's with me, how come it hurts so bad? How come it hurts so bad inside?"

"Well, Mike, Corky's just trying to get comfortable in his new home."

Mike didn't understand. "What new home?"

"Corky's a part of you now. He lives in your heart."

Mike cried a little more, because it still hurt. Then Mike decided that if Corky couldn't sleep on his head anymore, his heart wasn't such a bad place for him to be.

In his head, he told Corky he was sorry he'd ever been angry at him.

He told him that the Forever Plan was still going to work, only a little differently than he'd expected.

Then he let Corky all the way into his heart.
And it felt warm inside.